The Little Spotted Unicorn

Coloring Book

A Little Coyote Story

NM Reed

&

McCarthy Preston

Illustrations by

NM Reed

Njla Shojaie

JD Soriano

The Little Spotted Unicorn

Coloring Book

A Little Coyote Story

"Hi! I'm Sugar, the Story-telling Pony! Let me tell you a story!"

You rarely see Unicorns anymore, they hide where no one would think to look.

Pearl and Splash were big and beautiful and shining.
By day they hide in the forest in the brightest of sunbeams.

By night, the owl brought them dreams of their own baby unicorn fawn.

Baby Unicorn fawns were the cutest of all things!

arl and Splash were waiting for the birth of their fawn. It began to rain.
One of the other mothers come running toward them in the meadow.

"Help us, Splash! The babies are caught in the river!"
she cried as the sky grew dark, and the rain fell.
He ran to the river and saw the babies
stranded on a rock way out in the middle.

Splash waded in deep, and called to the baby unicorns,
"Here! Jump on my back! Hold on tight!"

Splash swam back to where the others were waiting.

The babies were safe, but Splash could not see Pearl.
He looked high, and low, and here and there.
But Pearl could not be found anywhere.

Just then he saw Pearl, hiding among the trees.
He ran up, he couldn't wait!
But what's that? Her four legs had turned into eight!

Pearl had her new fawn shining and brand new.
He could see him standing there in the cold morning dew.

"I saw tiny human and her little dog, reading her little book,
there upon a log. The dog stepped up and touched me on the face.
And all the magic it did erase."

Patches the no-horn unicorn played in the grass.

At night they slept together in the forest,
with the night watch owl swooping by overhead.

Until one day he grew big and strong,
and it was time for him to go out on his own.

The wild horses of the plains, where all plain unicorns go,
found him there and took him off to the land of rain and snow.

The little spotted Unicorn with no horn named Patches
grew up to have a band of wild horses of his own.

Then all the animals gathered in the barn for a good night's rest.

"Bye-Bye, now! Thanks for listening!"

The Littlest Coyote Falls In Love

The Littlest Coyote Falls in Love

The Littlest Coyote loved riding in the car
with his child, and with Cody Coyote
drooling out the other side of the car.

"Hi! I'm Flowers the Donkey." The Littlest Coyote said to his new frien "What wonderful big ears you have.

She stood there with no defense
as Coyote suddenly leaped the fence.
The Littlest Coyote and Flowers the Donkey

The Littlest Coyote and Flowers the Donke

The Howling Haloween Pumpkin

The Howling Haloween Pumpkin

THE
LITTLEST
COYOTE
CHRISTMAS

The Littlest Coyote climbed up the roof to the top.
He pulled his leg and Santa came out with a "Pop!!"
The Littlest Coyote and the

Clown Train to Playtime Toy Town
The Littlest Coyote Christmas 2

THE LITTLEST COYOTE

The Little Spotted Unicorn
The Little Spotted Unicorn